For Polawee

SIMON & SCHUSTER BOOKS FOR YOUNG READERS
An imprint of Simon & Schuster Children's Publishing Division
1230 Avenue of the Americas, New York, New York 10020
Copyright © 2016 by Susie Lee Jin

For information about special discounts for bulk purchases, please contact Simon & Schuster Special Sales
at 1-866-506-1949 or business@simonandschuster.com.

The Simon & Schuster Speakers Bureau can bring authors to your live event.
For more information or to book an event, contact the Simon & Schuster Speakers Bureau at 1-866-248-3049
or visit our website at www.simonspeakers.com.

Book design by Lucy Ruth Cummins
The text for this book is set in Graham.
The illustrations for this book are rendered in gouache and watercolor pencils.
Manufactured in China
1015 SCP
2 4 6 8 10 9 7 5 3 1

Library of Congress Cataloging-in-Publication Data
Jin, Susie Lee, author.
Mine! / by Susie Lee Jin ; illustrated by Susie Lee Jin. — 1st edition.
pages cm
Summary: A humorous picture book about a group of bunnies fighting over a big juicy carrot.
ISBN 978-1-4814-2772-2 (hardcover) — ISBN 978-1-4814-2773-9 (ebook)
[1. Rabbits—Fiction. 2. Carrots—Fiction. 3. Humorous stories.] I. Title.
PZ7.J575258 Mi 2016
1. Rabbits—Juvenile fiction. 2. Carrots—Juvenile fiction.
[E]—dc23
2014036331

first edition

MINE!

SUSIE LEE JIN

SIMON & SCHUSTER BOOKS FOR YOUNG READERS

New York   London   Toronto   Sydney   New Delhi

Mine.

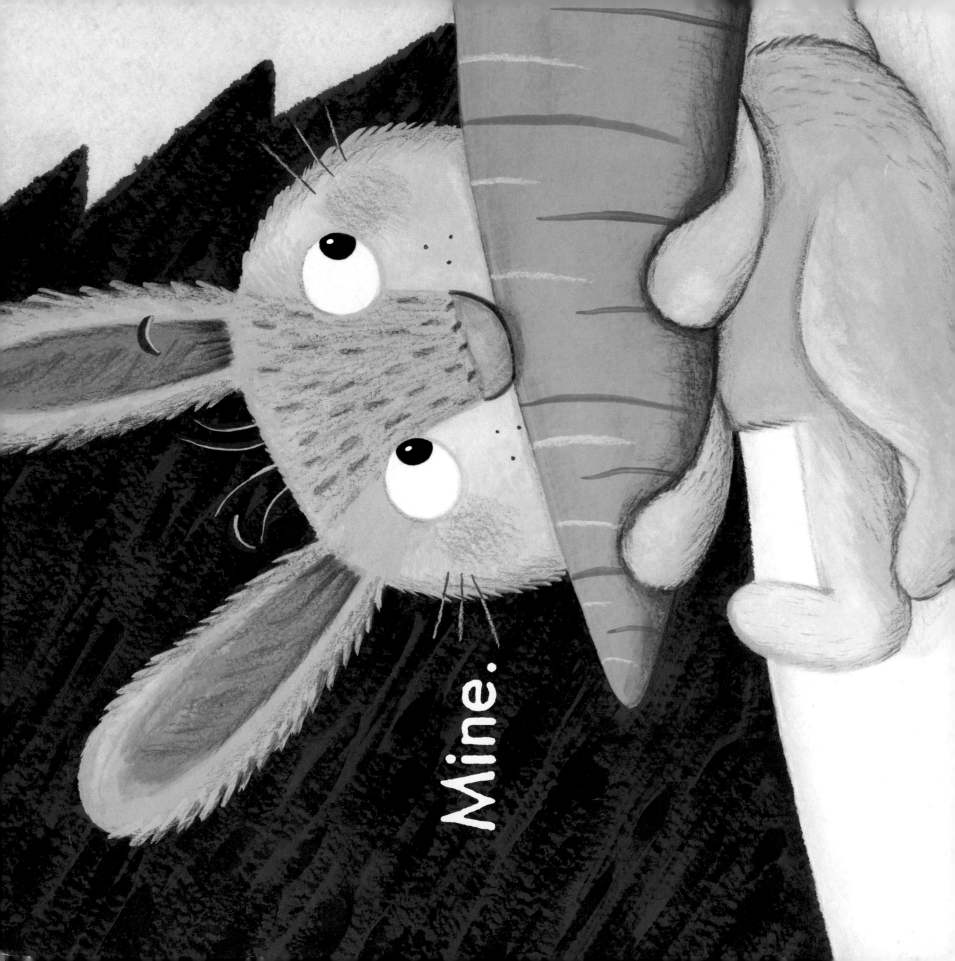

Mine!

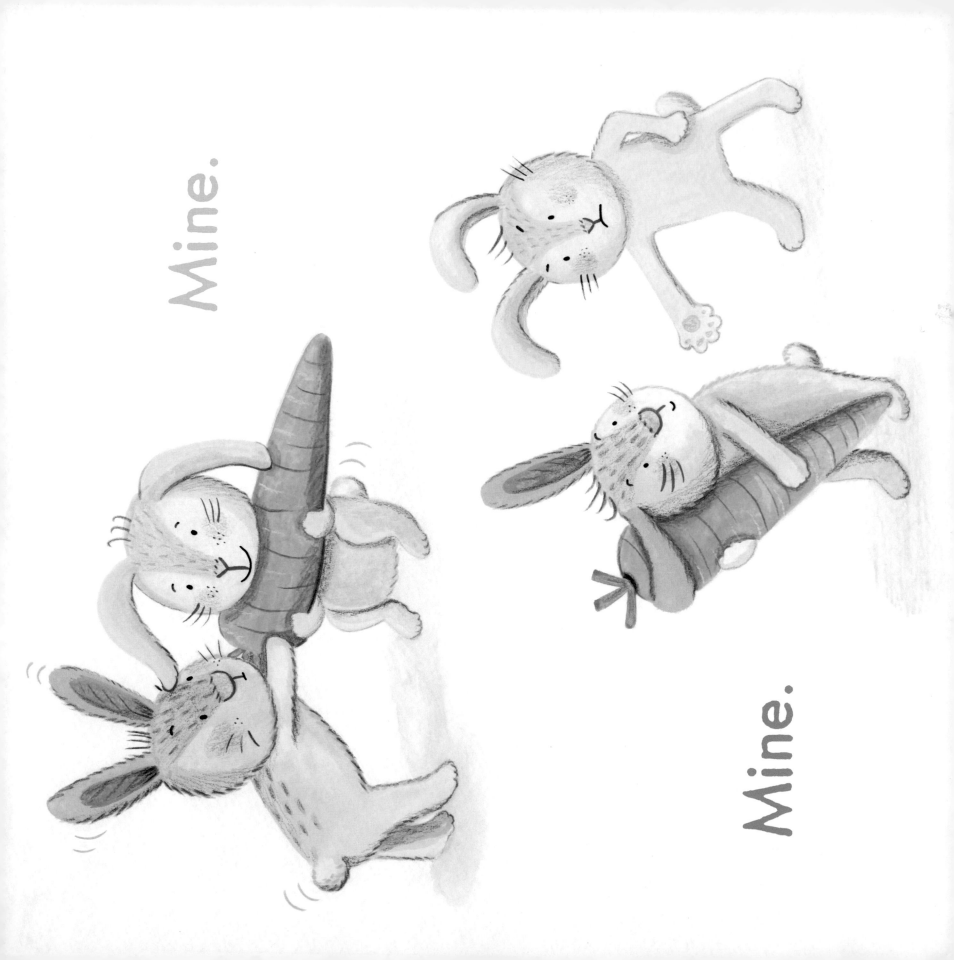

Mine.

Mine.

Mine!

Mine.

Mine!

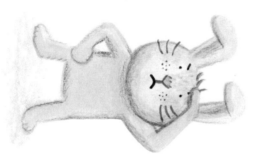

Mine!

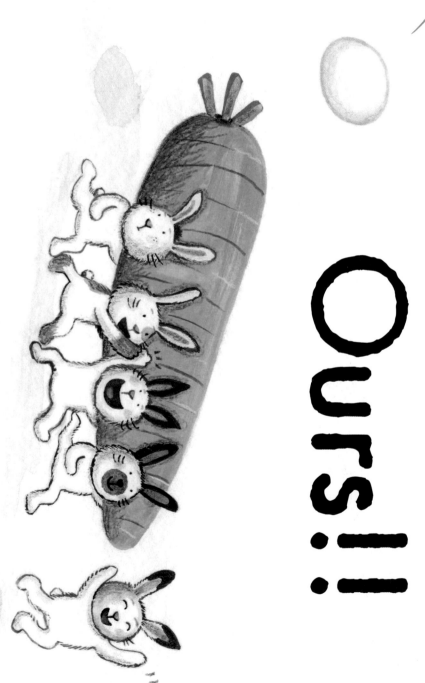

Ours!!

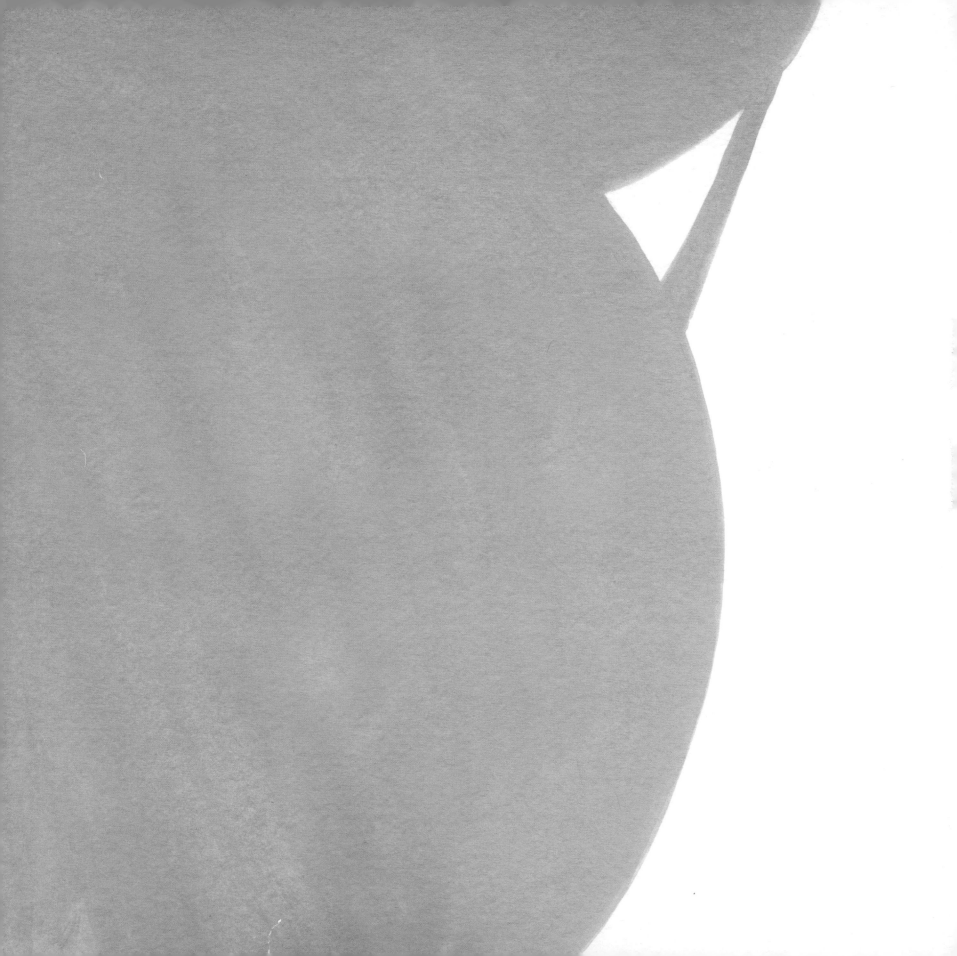

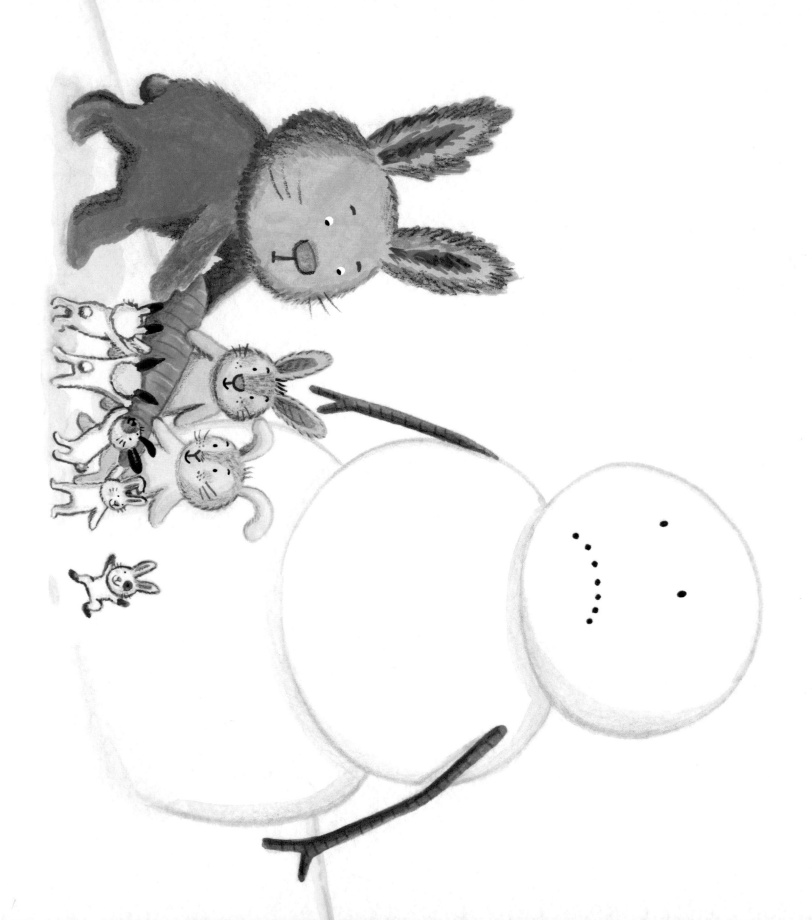

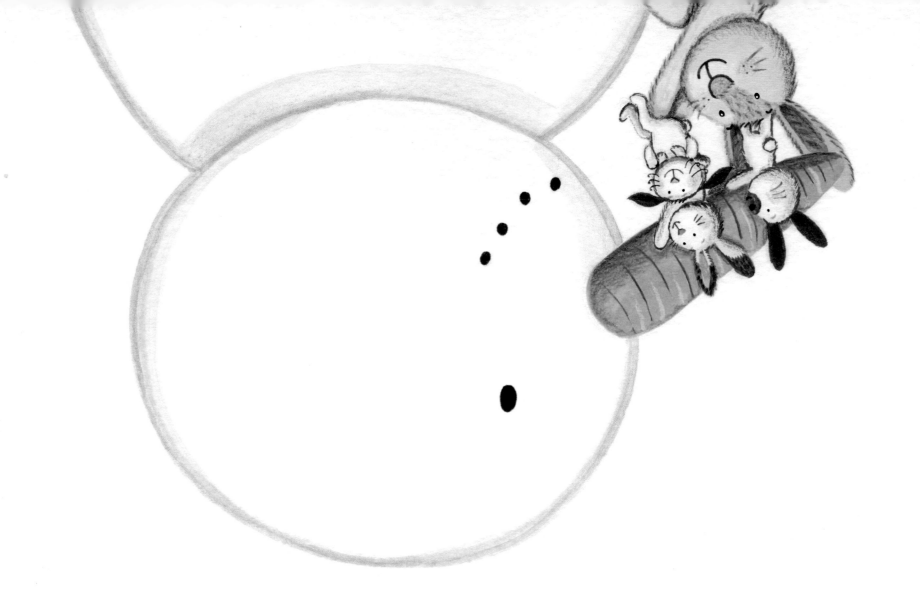

yours.

Mine.